MOLLYCODDLE

THE TALE OF PAMPERED GIRL

CATHERINE NITHISHA C

Made with ❤ on the Notion Press Platform
www.notionpress.com

I give thanks to God for fulfilling my desire! I am so grateful that my first book, "Mollycoddle," has been published. I want to express my sincere gratitude to everyone who has helped me along the way. Your constant support, direction, and affection have been the inspiration for this book. I want to express my gratitude to my mother, sisters, brothers, family, friends, well-wishers, and readers for supporting me and my tale. I will always be thankful for your support, which means the world to me. I would especially like to thank the college's (DACE) distinguished faculties and helpful personnel. "I appreciate your assistance in making 'Mollycoddle' a reality."

Contents

Foreword

Dear Reader,

Anna, a girl born into a loving family in Texas, is the subject of the touching tale "The Tale of Pampered Girl." With the help of her grandfather, Mark, Jane, who lost her father when she was a little girl, raises her and her older sister, Rachel. Despite being bullied and experiencing emotional difficulties, Anna aspires to be a doctor. She is forced to enroll in an engineering institution after being psychologically devastated by the death of her grandfather prior to her medical admission exam. With the help of her friends and family, she regains her self-esteem, succeeds professionally, and gives her mother a lavish lifestyle. After getting married to Jaden, Anna eventually achieves her goal of becoming a prosperous doctor.

Preface

The Tale of a Pampered Girl is the heartfelt journey of Anna, a young girl born into a loving family in Texas. Raised by her mother, Jane, and her supportive grandfather, Mark, Anna faces the challenges of growing up without a father. Alongside her older sister, Rachel, Anna navigates the complexities of life, marked by bullying and emotional struggles. Despite these obstacles, Anna dreams of becoming a doctor, driven by a deep desire to help others.

However, life takes an unexpected turn when her grandfather passes away just before Anna is set to take her medical entrance exam, leaving her emotionally shattered. As a result, Anna is forced to enroll in an engineering institution, a decision that seems to diverge from her original dream. But with the unwavering support of her friends and family, she rebuilds her confidence, rediscovering her strength and determination. Through perseverance, she not only succeeds in her professional life but also provides her mother with the lavish lifestyle she deserves.

In time, Anna marries Jaden, and with her relentless spirit, she finally achieves her dream of becoming a successful doctor. This story is a testament to the power of resilience, the importance of family, and the strength to overcome life's hardest trials to achieve one's dreams.

Acknowledgements

I would like to express my deepest gratitude to the following individuals whose love, encouragement, and unwavering support have been instrumental in the completion of this book.

To my beloved mother, C Jenifer Rajasekar, whose endless love, guidance, and sacrifices have shaped me into who I am today. Your strength and nurturing spirit continue to inspire me every day.

To my dear sisters, C Rathisha Rajasekar and Anusha, for your constant support and for being my pillars of strength. Your belief in me has been a source of motivation throughout this journey.

To my cherished friend, Jafrein, whose friendship and encouragement have been invaluable. Your support has made this journey even more meaningful.

To my brothers, A Abdul Rahman and M Abdullah, thank you for always standing by me with love and encouragement. Your presence in my life is a true blessing.

I am immensely grateful to the supportive faculties who have helped me at every step: Mr. Elayaraja, whose wisdom and guidance have been instrumental, and the esteemed Dr. J. Rahila Ma'am and Mr. Paramasivam Sir, for their constant support, mentorship, and belief in my work.

Finally, to all those who have touched my life in ways both big and small, thank you. This book is as much yours as it is mine.

Prologue

Anna's story begins in the heart of Texas, where she was born into a family full of love and warmth. Raised by her devoted mother, Jane, and her wise grandfather, Mark, Anna's life was shaped by their unwavering support after the loss of her father when she was just a little girl. Alongside her older sister, Rachel, Anna grew up learning the values of strength and resilience.

Despite facing relentless bullying and emotional challenges, Anna harbored a dream of becoming a doctor. Her heart was set on healing others, but fate had other plans. Just before her medical entrance exam, tragedy struck—her beloved grandfather passed away, leaving Anna shattered. Grief-stricken and lost, she was forced to enroll in an engineering institution, a path that seemed far from the future she had once envisioned.

But even in her darkest moments, Anna's family and friends stood by her side. Their support helped her rediscover her strength and reignite the self-esteem she had lost. With time, Anna not only overcame the hurdles life threw her way but also found success in her career, ultimately giving her mother the lavish lifestyle she had always dreamed of.

In the end, after marrying Jaden, Anna's journey culminated in the realization of her deepest ambition—becoming a prosperous doctor. The Tale of a Pampered Girl is a story of perseverance, love, and the power of believing in oneself, even when life seems to steer you off course.

CHAPTER ONE

"THE PLACE OF PRIVILEGE" (INTRODUCTION TO ANNA'S PAMPERED LIFE)

(PLACE: MARCO HOSPITAL, TEXAS).

On a radiant morning, as the sun rose over Texas, casting a warm yellow glow over Marco Hospital, Jane's contractions intensified. Clutching her swollen belly, she breathed deeply, her husband Steve by her side.

"Almost there, my girl," Steve whispered, holding her hand. Jane nodded her head, her eyes locked on the monitor tracking their baby's heartbeat. Dr. Rosie entered, smiling reassuringly. On the contrary, Mark and Sarah (Steve's parents) are waiting outside the labor ward. Mark (Steve's dad) sat nervously flipping through a magazine.

"Any news?" Mark asked his younger son John (Steve's brother), "Not yet," John replied, "but Steve will update us soon." Sarah worriedly glanced at her watch. "It's taking too long." The little girl Rachel, the firstborn of Jane and Steve, paced outside the labor ward, her excitement building with each passing minute. She couldn't wait to meet her little sibling. "How much longer?" Rachel asked her grandparents, Mark and Sarah, for the umpteenth time. Sarah smiled patiently at Rachel, "Soon, sweetie, the doctor will let us know!" Rachel nodded. Steve had promised to text updates of the condition of Jane in the labor ward, so Sarah was checking her phone for what felt like the hundredth time. As Sarah and Rachel walked back to the waiting room, Rachel noticed a nursery rhyme poster on the wall: "WELCOME LITTLE ONE, SWEET AND SMALL, A BUNDLE OF JOY, FOR ONE AND ALL," and eagerly asked her grandma what was in that baby's poster, and Sarah explained in her own understanding language, After hearing that, Rachel's heart swelled with love and anticipation. Rachel imagined holding her little sibling, playing with her, and teaching her.

On the other side, Jane (Rachel's mom) is struggling inside the labor ward. Nurses bustled around, prepping the delivery room.

Jane's water broke...

"Time to meet your little one!" Dr. Rosy Announced with a hardship due to the final surge of energy, Jane gave birth to a tiny, crying bundle of joy.

"Congratulations, you have a beautiful baby girl!" Dr. Rosy exclaimed.

The nurse cut the umbilical cord as Jane cradled their daughter in her arms, beaming at Steve. Tears of joy streaming down her face, Jane gazed at Steve. "She's perfect!" Steve smiled and said, "Our second little princess has arrived."

As baby's first cries filled the room, the family members were awaiting for the arrival of their new addition. Amidst the anticipation, the grandparents had their hearts set on a baby boy. As they waited, the hospital's intercom system crackled, and a gentle voice announced, "Baby girl born to Mr. and Mrs. Steve, Room: 304."

The family exchanged excited smiles. Mark and Sarah rushed to the labor ward, followed by John (Rachel's uncle). Suddenly, Steve emerged from the labor ward, beaming.

"Rachel'! You have a little sister!" he exclaimed. Rachel became happy, and her eyes widened with excitement. "Is Mom okay? What's little girl like?'.

Steve chuckled, "Mom is amazing, and the little one's perfect; you'll definitely love her." Rachel rushed to the labor ward, almost bouncing with excitement. As Rachel entered into the labor ward, Jane smiled, cradling the little one in her arms.

"Meet your little sister," Jane said, tears shining in her eyes.

Rachel had been waiting for this moment for what felt like forever. Rachel's gaze locked onto the little bundle, and her heart melted. "Oh, baby girl," she whispered, her voice trembling with emotion. Rachel approached the bed cautiously, not counting on startling the little girl as she peered into the blanket. The little girl's big, round eyes stared back at her. Rachel's heart skipped a beat.

"Hi, baby girl!" Rachel gently stroked the little girl's soft hair. The little girl wrapped her tiny fingers around Rachel's index finger, holding on tight. Rachel giggled, "You're so small and cute!" She exclaimed, marveling at her button nose and rosebud lips. Jane handed Rachel a small, soft toy.

"Want to give little girl as her first gift?" Rachel asked.

Jane replied, 'No sweetheart, it's for you.'.

Rachel smiles, and her eyes light up. "Yeah!" she gently placed the toy near the baby, who grasped it instinctively. As Rachel watched Anna sleep, she felt an overwhelming sense of love and responsibility. She was going to be an amazing big sister!.

Jane's heart swelled with emotion as she wanted Rachel to meet the baby for the first time. She had dreamt of this moment, envisioning the instant when her two daughters would connect. As Rachel gently stroked Anna's hair, Jane felt tears prick at the corners of her eyes. She was overwhelmed with love and gratitude, knowing that her family was now complete. Steve sat beside Jane, wrapping his arm around her shoulder." Smiling at the tender scene unfolding before them. Jane leaned into Steve, feeling his warmth and support. She watched as Rachel and the newborn baby bonded, their hearts. Connecting in a way that transcended words. As the nurse helped Jane settle the newborn baby into her crib, Rachel snuggled up beside her, holding the baby's tiny hand. Jane's heart overflowed with joy, seeing her two daughters together.

Steve snapped photos, capturing the precious moments. "Our little family is perfect!" he whispered, beaming with joy. Jane smiled, feeling a deep sense of contentment. "We're complete," she agreed, gazing at Rachel and the newborn baby. As they sat together basking in the warmth of their newfound love, Jane knew that this moment would forever be etched in her memory—a snapshot of pure joy, love, and perfection.

The first few days passed in a blissful blur. Jane, Steve, Rachel, and the baby settled into a cozy routine. Jane and Steve took turns caring for the baby, feeding, changing, and cuddling her. Rachel revealed in her new role as big sister. She helped with small tasks, like fetching diapers or singing lullabies to newborn babies. Jane and Steve marveled at Rachel's gentle, nurturing side. On the third day, Jane and Steve decided to be discharged from the hospital. Rachel bounded with excitement; Jane and Steve strolled hand in hand, enjoying the warm sunshine and fresh air. As they sat on a blanket, watching Rachel play with the newborn baby, Jane turned to Steve. "This is perfect," she whispered, her eyes shining with happiness. Steve smiled, wrapping his arm around Jane. We're a family," he said, his voice filled with emotion. In that moment, surrounded by the people she loved most, Jane knew that life couldn't get better. On the other side, Mark and Sarah, Rachel's grandparents, were over the moon with excitement as they awaited the arrival of their new grandchild. They had been eagerly anticipating this moment for months, and the countdown had finally come to an end. As they prepared to meet their new grandbaby, Mark and Sarah couldn't help but feel a mix of emotions. They were thrilled at the prospect of welcoming a new addition to their family, but they were also a little nervous about how Rachel would adjust to having a new sitting. "We hope Rachel will be a good big sister," Sarah said to Mark as they sat in their cozy living room, surrounded by photos of Rachel's childhood.

"Of course, she will," Mark replied, smiling confidently. Rachel is a kind and caring child; she'll love having a new sibling to look after." Mark and Sarah had a special bond with their first granddaughter, and they were eager to form a similar bond with their new grandchild. As they imagined their future with the new baby. Mark and Sarah envisioned lazy Sundays spent playing with the kids, family vacations to the beach, and cozy nights spent reading bedtime stories.

"We're going to spoil this baby rotten," Sarah said, laughing.

"That's our job as grandparents, Mark replied, chuckling.

And on a fine day, the whole family gathered in the living room, surrounded by baby books, papers, and pens. Jane and Steve sat on the couch with the baby snuggled up between them, while Rachel sat on the floor, playing with her toys. Mark and Sarah sat in their favorite armchairs, looking excited and eager to start the discussion.

"Okay, let's get started!" Jane said, smiling at everyone. "We need to find the perfect name for our little baby girl."

"I think we should name her something classic and timeless, "Sarah suggested, like Victoria or Elizabeth. "I like those names, Steve said.

"But I was thinking something a bit more unique. Like Helen or Adlin.

Rachel looked up from her toys. "I like the name Anna, "she said. " It's pretty and simple. Jane smiled at Rachel. "We're actually thinking of keeping Anna as her middle name," she explained. "We need to find a first name that goes well with it."

Mark pulled out a piece of paper and started scribbling down names. "How about Sophia Anna? He suggested, "Olivia Anna?"

As the discussion went on, the room was filled with laughter and debate. Everyone had their own opinions and suggestions, but they all agreed on one thing: they wanted a name that was perfect for their little girl.

After what felt like hours of discussion, Jane looked around the room and smiled. "I think we're getting close," she said. Let's make a list of our top three names, and then we can decide from there.

The family worked together to narrow down their options, and finally, they had their top three names: Sophia Anna, Olivia Anna, and Josh Anna.

As they sat around the room, looking at their list, Jane turned to Steve and smiled," I think we're ready to make a decision," she said.

Steve nodded, looking at their little girl who was sleeping peacefully in Jane's arms. And with that, the family made their decision. They chose a name that they all loved, a name that was Josh Anna, and it's perfect for their little girl.

CHAPTER TWO

"SUGAR AND SPICE" (ANNA'S HAPPY AND SAD MOMENTS)

As the days went by, Anna grew into a happy and blessed child, surrounded by her loving family. Her sister took on the role of a mini-caregiver, helping with small tasks and showering Anna with affection. The sisters' bond grew stronger with each passing day, filling the house with laughter and sweetness." Anna's childhood was a tapestry of happy moments, woven together by the love and laughter of her family. Here are a few cherished memories.

As a toddler, Anna would spend hours playing with her big sister Rachel, building forts, etc. Their parents, Jane and Steve, would join in, making silly faces and voices to send the girls into fits of giggles. Summer afternoons were spent at the beach, where Rachel would build sandcastles with her dad and Jane used to read books under a colorful umbrella.

These happy moments, and many more like that, filled Anna's childhood with joy, love, and a sense of belonging to a wonderful family.

As Anna's "One year of love, laughter, and adventure!" The family was buzzing with excitement as they prepared for little Anna's first birthday celebration. The house was filled with the sweet scent of freshly baked cupcakes and the sound of upbeat music.

Jane, Anna's mom, was busy in the kitchen, whipping up a storm of colorful decorations and party favors. She carefully placed tiny pink and white flowers on the cupcake tower, making sure everything was perfect for her little princess.

Steve, Anna's dad, was setting up the backyard, inflating balloons and hanging streamers. He couldn't help but feel a sense of pride and joy, thinking about how fast his little girl had grown.

Rachel, Anna's big sister, was helping with the party preparations, carefully placing party hats on the tables and making sure the boxes were filled with candy.

She couldn't wait to celebrate her little sister's special day.

Meanwhile, Mark and Sarah, Anna's grandparents, were getting ready to arrive, bearing gifts and big smiles. They were thrilled to be a part of their special milestone in Anna's life.

As the family worked together to get everything ready, Anna herself was taking a nap, oblivious to all the excitement. But when she woke up, she would be surrounded by love, laughter, and all the joy of her very first birthday celebration. And they celebrated the birthday celebration of Anna as well as their firstborn Rachel's birthday celebration.

As the last guest departed and the final party favor was handed out, the family let out a collective sigh of happiness and exhaustion. The birthday party had been a resounding success, filled with laughter, love, and memories to cherish. Jane and Steve looked at each other, smiling wearily, as they surveyed the aftermath of the celebration. The house was quiet once again, except for the occasional creak of the old wooden floorboards. Rachel, Anna's big sister, was already fast asleep, her eyelids heavy with the weight of the day filled with excitement and fun. Mark and Sarah, the grandparents, had headed home, beaming with pride and joy, after a wonderful day spent with their loved ones.

As for little Anna, the birthday girl herself, she was sleeping peacefully in her crib, a soft smile on her face, surrounded by the reviews of her special day. Her first birthday had been a day to remember, and as she drifted off to sleep, she was surrounded by the love and adoration of her family.

As the night drew to a close, Jane and Steve exchanged a tender glance, feeling grateful for this little family of theirs and for the joy that they shared with full hearts and happy memories. They too drifted off to sleep, filled by the silence of the night and the knowledge that they had created a day that would be etched in their memories forever.

A few days after the joyous celebration of Anna's first birthday, but in an instant, their happy world was turned upside down. When Anna was just a year and a half old, and Rachel was 3.5 years old, tragedy struck; she lost her beloved father to health complications. The devastating blow left her family reeling, and their lives were forever changed. Her mother's strength and resilience were tested as she struggled to come to terms with the loss, while Anna's elder sister, who was just 3.5 years old, tried to make sense of the absence of her father, whom she adored.

Little Anna, too young to fully understand the permanence of death, missed the warm embrace and loving smile of her daddy, leaving a void in her little heart."

Anna was too young to comprehend the permanence of loss, and her tender mind couldn't grasp the concept of death. She didn't even remember her father's face or the joyful moments they shared. Her elder sister, only 3.5 years old and barely starting kindergarten, struggled to understand the absence of their father's warm presence. She couldn't fathom how to process her own grief, let alone support her little sister. The sister's world was turned upside down, leaving them with a sense of confusion, sadness, and a longing for the happy moments with their father they once had.

Anna's mother was consumed by grief, unable to come to terms with the loss of her partner. The pain was overwhelming, leaving her emotionally unstable and struggling to cope with the responsibilities of raising her two young daughters alone, feeling utterly broken.

Jane, the girl's mother, sat down with Rachel and Anna in a quiet corner of the living room, surrounded by photos and memories of their father. She took a deep breath, trying to find the right words to explain the situation to her young daughters. "Babies, you know how sometimes people we love get sick or hurt, and we have to take care of them?" Jane began, looking at Rachel, who nodded solemnly.

"Well, Daddy was very sick, and his body stopped working," Jane continued, trying to use simple and honest language.

"That means he won't be able to come back and play with us or give us hugs and kisses."

Rachel's eyes swelled up with tears, and she looked at her mother with a mix of sadness and confusion. "But why, Mommy?" she asked, her voice trembling. Jane pulled Rachel into a tight hug. We can't help; their body just gets too tired, and they have to go to a special place where they can rest and be happy,'" she explained.

Anna, who had been quietly observing the conversation, suddenly looked up at her mother with big, curious eyes. "Daddy gone?" she asked, her voice barely above a whisper.

Jane nodded, tears streaming down her face. "Yes, baby, Daddy is gone. But we'll always remember him, and we'll take care of each other, okay?"

Rachel and Anna both nodded their heads, still looking confused and sad, but also a little reassured by their mother's words. Jane hugged both of them tightly, holding them close as they navigated this difficult and painful time together.

The beautiful family had been turned dark, and they had to move forward, one difficult step at a time. The memory of Steve's love and laughter would stay with them forever, but for now they had to find a new sense of normalcy. In the aftermath of Steve's passing, Anna's family struggled to come to terms with the loss. Jane, Anna's mother, was consumed by grief, but she knew she had to stay strong for her daughters. She made a conscious effort to maintain a sense of normalcy and routine, even as she navigated her own emotions. Anna, being only a year old, didn't fully understand the concept of death, but she sensed the changes in her family's dynamics. She became more clingy and demanding of attention, which Jane patiently provided. Jane made sure to maintain a sense of continuity and familiarity for Anna, sticking to regular routines and rituals. Janes's relationship with Rachel and Anna evolved as they navigated their grief together. She became more patient, understanding, and empathetic, recognizing that each of her daughters was processing their loss in their own unique way.

Despite Jane's best efforts, she struggled to come to terms with the gaping void left by his absence. Jane's world had been shattered by the sudden loss of her beloved husband; every waking moment felt like an uphill battle as she tried to navigate the treacherous terrain of grief.

At first, Jane put on a brave face, determined to be strong for her daughters, Rachel and Anna. She went through the motions of daily life and attending to her daughter's needs. But beneath the surface, she was drowning in a sea of despair.

As the days turned into weeks, Jane's façade began to crack. She found herself breaking down in tears. The memories of Steve lingered in every corner of their house, making it impossible for her to escape the pain.

Jane tried to find solace in her relationships with her daughters, but even those interactions felt hollow, without them by her side. Despite her best efforts, Jane couldn't shake off the feeling of emptiness that had settled in her heart. She felt like a part of her had been amputated, leaving her with a constant ache that couldn't be soothed.

In a desperate bid to provide her daughters with a sense of resemblance to stability, Jane made the difficult decision to send them to kindergarten, even though Anna was only 1.5 years old. Rachel, who was a few years older, would be able to provide some support and comfort to her little sister, Jane hoped.

She felt a pang of guilt and sadness. She knew that she wasn't in a good place, mentally or emotionally, and that her daughters deserved better.

But she also knew that she had to take care of herself, if only for their kids sake. With a heavy heart, Jane knew that she had made a difficult but necessary decision.

CHAPTER THREE

"REBELLION IN SILK SHOES" (ANNA'S INDULGENCES)

Little Anna began her educational journey at the tender age of 1.5, surrounded by the warmth and love of her family. Despite the absence of her father, her life was filled with joy and contentment, and the unwavering support of her paternal family, her grandparents, aunts, and uncles became her pillars of strength, ensuring that Anna and her elder sister felt loved and cherished. Together, they created a nurturing environment that helped the sisters thrive, shielding them from the harsh realities of life.

CATHERINE NITHISHA C

Meanwhile, Anna thrived in kindergarten. She made new friends, learned new things, and grew more confident with each passing day. But despite her happy exterior, Anna's family knew that she had experienced a profound loss at a very young age. She had never really known her father, and as a result, she had missed out on the unconditional love and support that only a father can provide.

To compensate for this loss, Steve's family pampered Anna even more than her sister Rachel. They showered her with love, attention, and affection, hoping to fill the void left by her father's absence. And as Anna grew old, she began to sense that she was being treated differently, that she was given more attention and more love than her sister.

As Anna transitioned to nursery school, she was excited to start a new chapter in her life. She had grown up a lot since kindergarten, and she was eager to make new friends and learn new things. And as luck would have it. She was reunited with a childhood friend from kindergarten, someone who had been a presence in her life since she was a toddler.

Years went by, and Anna became a 6-year-old kid promoted from nursery school into her primary school classroom. She couldn't help but feel a mix of excitement and nerves; she had grown up so much since kindergarten, and she was eager to start this new chapter in her life. As the days turned into weeks, Anna began to blossom in primary school. She grew more confident.

Anna's education was also a top priority. She attended a prestigious primary school, where she was caught by caring teachers.

Anna's social life was also filled with fun and exciting activities. At home, Anna was treated to a life of luxury. She and her grandparents would spoil her with treats and gifts.

Despite being pampered, Anna was not a spoiled child. She was kind, gentle, and respectful, always saying please and thank you; her family's love and attention had taught her the importance of gratitude and humility.

Jane, Anna's mom, faced numerous struggles as a single parent. After losing her husband, Jane was left to care for their young daughters on her own. The grief and sadness of Steve's loss were overwhelming, but she knew she had to be strong for her daughter's sake. One of the biggest challenges Jane faced was financial instability. Steve's passing left Jane with a significant reduction in income. She had to work multiple jobs to make ends meet, often leaving her daughters in the care of her in-laws.

Despite her best efforts, Jane struggled to balance work and parenting responsibilities. There were many days when Jane felt like she was barely holding it together, and the weight of her responsibilities as a single parent felt crushing.

Anna was blessed with a loving family, but her grandfather Mark held a special place in her heart. He was her rock, her confidant, and her favorite person in the whole world; little Anna adored him with all her might, and he reciprocated her love with unconditional affection. Although she never experienced the love of a father, her grandfather's pure and selfless love filled that void, showing her what it meant to be loved unconditionally. His gentle guidance, warm embraces, and kind words made her feel seen, heard, and cherished. In her grandfather's eyes, Anna saw a love that was unwavering, a love that made her feel like she was home.

Like a beautiful butterfly emerging from its cocoon, Anna blossomed into a bright and ambitious young girl.

A decade had passed, and the once little Anna had grown into a confident and determined individual. As she entered secondary school, her goals crystallized, and she set her heart on becoming a doctor with unwavering dedication. She threw herself into her studies, driven by a singular passion to make her mother's sacrifices and love. She was determined to prove herself, not just as a talented student but also as a compassionate and skilled healer, making a difference in the lives.

On one random day,

Anna walked into her school on her 13th birthday; she felt like she was on the top of the world. She was wearing her favorite new dress, her hair was styled perfectly by her mom, and she had a big smile on her face. She was excited to celebrate her special day with her friends and classmates.

But as she walked into her classroom, Anna's excitement was quickly dampened by one of her classmates, a girl who had always been jealous of Anna's father. "Hey everyone, did you know that Anna's father is dead?" the girl said loud enough for the whole class to hear.

Anna felt like she had been punched in the gut. She couldn't believe that someone would say something so hurtful and insensitive on her birthday. She tried to hold back tears, but they began to flow anyway.

The teacher quickly stepped in and warned the girl to apologize and behave. But the damage was already done. Anna was devastated, and no amount of consolation from teachers or her friends could stop her tears.

As the day went on, Anna struggled to focus on her schoolwork. She felt like she was in a daze, and the pain of her classmate's words lingered. She couldn't wait to get out of school and go home to her family, who would surely comfort her and make her feel better.

When the final bell rang, Anna quickly gathered her things and rushed out of the classroom. She didn't stop crying. As the school van rumbled home, Anna settled into her usual window seat, her tears still flowing freely. The wind rushing in through the open window carried her tears away, and some of them landed on Rachel, who was sitting beside her.

Rachel looked up at Anna, concern etched on her face. "Anna, what happened?"

But Anna didn't respond. She just continued to cry, her body shaking with sobs. Rachel had never seen her sister like this before. Anna was always the strong and confident one, and Rachel was shocked to see her so vulnerable. Rachel's eyes welled up with tears as she looked at Anna. She didn't know what was wrong, but she knew that her sister was hurting; without thinking, Rachel reached out and wrapped her arms around Anna, holding her close as they both cried together.

Rachel had never seen Anna cry like this before, and she didn't know how to react. But Rachel just held her sister, trying to comfort her as they rode home in silence, their little hearts heavy with emotion.

Jane stood at the bus stop, eagerly waiting for her daughters to arrive. She had a big smile on her face, expecting to see Anna's bright smile and Rachel's bubbly personality as they stepped off the bus, but as the bus doors opened, Jane's smile faltered. Anna and Rachel walked off the bus, both of them crying uncontrollably. Jane's heart sank as she rushed to envelop her daughters in a warm hug.

"Hey, my babies, what's wrong?" Jane asked, trying to keep her voice calm and soothing. They cried harder, unable to speak. Jane gently guided them towards the house, trying to comfort them as they walked. As they entered the house, "Tell me, what happened?" Jane asked, in a soft and gentle voice, Anna slowly lifted her head, her eyes red and puffy from crying, "I...... I was made fun of at school, "Anna stammered, her voice shaking. Rachel looked up at Jane, her eyes welling up with tears again. " Someone said something about Daddy and mocked, "Anna by saying she is fatherless." Rachel added, her voice barely above a whisper.

Jane was shocked and outraged when she heard what had happened. Jane consoled them, but Anna couldn't shake the feeling that her classmate's cruel words had ruined her special day forever.

She had refused to go to school for two days, still reeling from the hurtful comment made by her classmate. But after a relaxing weekend with her family, Anna felt like she was ready to face her fears and return to school.

As the days turned into weeks and the weeks into months, Anna continued to thrive in her secondary school. She consistently earned top grades, impressing her teachers and parents with her academic progress. Her confidence grew with each passing day, and she began to see herself as a capable and intelligent individual.

Anna was still the pampered kid, with her mother and sister doting on her every need. Jane continued to work hard to provide for her daughters. The three of them formed a tight-knit unit, supporting and loving each other through thick and thin.

As Anna approached the end of her secondary school journey, she began to think about her future. She had always been fascinated by the medical field, and she had decided that she wanted to become a doctor. The thought of helping others, of making a difference in people's lives, excited and motivated her.

CHAPTER FOUR

"WORLD OUTSIDE" (INTRODUCING THE INCITING INCIDENT / CONFLICT)

Anna stepped into her 1st day of higher secondary school with a spring in her step and a confident smile on her face. She was determined to make the most of her two years of higher secondary education. As she settled into her new classroom, Anna's eyes scanned the room, taking in the familiar faces of her friends and classmates. She felt a sense of excitement and anticipation knowing that the next two years would be crucial in shaping her future. Anna's focus was laser sharp as she began her higher secondary journey. She was determined to score well in her final exams, knowing that it would open doors to top medical colleges and university exams.

As the initial nervousness of being in a new class began to wear off, Anna started to strike up conversations with her new classmates. She was excited to make new classmates. As she turned to talk to the girl sitting next to her, Anna's eyes widened in surprise. It was the same girl who had mocked her on her birthday in primary school. Anna had never forgotten the incident, but she had long since moved on.

The girl, whose name was Sophia, looked up at Anna with a mixture of nervousness and recognition. "Anna?" she asked, her voice tentative.

Anna nodded, and Sophia took a deep breath before speaking.

"I want to apologize for what I did on your birthday all those years ago," Sophi said, her eyes sincere, "I was a stupid kid, and I didn't realize how hurtful my words were. I've grown up a lot since then; I realize now that what I did was wrong." Anna was taken aback by Sophia's apology, she had never expected to see the girl again, let alone have her apologize for her past behavior. "It's okay," Anna said, smiling. "I've long since forgotten about it. But thank you for apologizing. It means a lot to me, Sophia smiled back, relief across her face. "I'm glad I would apologize," she said, "And I'm glad we can start fresh. I'd love to get to know you better, Anna."

As the days turned into weeks, Anna and Sophia proved to be loyal and trustworthy friends, always there to lend a listening ear or a helping hand. Anna appreciated her kindness and empathy, and she was grateful to have Sophia by her side.

Together, Anna and Sophia navigated and supported each other every step of the way.

Anna's teenage years were shaping up to be an incredible journey of growth, learning, and self-discovery. She was surrounded by loving people, exciting opportunities, and a sense of possibility that filled her with joy and anticipation for the future.

Anna and her sister Rachel shared a beautiful and supportive relationship. Despite their age difference, they were incredibly close, and Rachel had always been a role model and source of inspiration for Anna.

Rachel, being the elder sister, had always taken on a mentorship role in Anna's life; she would often share her own experiences, offering valuable advice and guidance on everything from academics to friendships.

Anna looked up to Rachel and admired her intelligence, confidence, and independence. As Rachel pursued her higher education at university, Anna would often seek her advice on her own academic pursuits. Rachel would share her own study tips. Anna cherished their moments, not only because she valued Rachel's input but also because it brought them closer together.

The sisters would often spend hours talking on the phone, sharing stories, and laughing together. Rachel would regale Anna with tales of her university adventures, from crazy professors to wild parties. Anna, in turn, would share her own high school experiences, from friendships to academics. Their conversations were always filled with laughter, love, and a deep understanding of each other. One of the things that Anna admired most about Rachel was her confidence and self-assurance. Rachel had always been someone who knew what she wanted and wasn't afraid to go after it. Anna aspired to be like her sister, to have that same level of confidence and determination.

In return, Rachel admired Anna's kindness, empathy, and comparison. Anna had a way of making everyone feel seen and heard, and Rachel cherished that about her sister.

Overall, the relationship between Anna and Rachel was built on a foundation of love, trust, and mutual respect. They were best friends, confidants, and partners in crime.

Anna and her grandfather shared a truly special and endearing relationship. They were incredibly close, and Anna cherished the time she spent with him.

Her grandpa, with his kind eyes and warm smile, had a way of making Anna feel seen and heard. He would listen to her for hours, asking thoughtful questions and offering words of wisdom. Anna felt like she could tell him anything, and he would always offer guidance and support without judgment. Her daily routine was a carefully curated schedule of indulgences; Anna's determination to become a doctor only grew stronger with each passing day.

Days went, she was now in the final stretch of her higher secondary education, and she was laser-focused on acing her final exams. But she wasn't just stopping at that; she was also simultaneously preparing for the highly competitive medical entrance exams. Anna's mom, Jane, was her rock, working tirelessly to support her daughter's dreams. She would often wake up early in the morning to help Anna with her studies, making sure she had everything she needed to succeed. Jane's hard work and sacrifices didn't go unnoticed, and Anna was deeply grateful for her mom's unwavering support.

The entire family was rallied behind Anna, cheering her on every step of the way. Her sister Rachel, who was already in university, would share her valuable advice and encouragement. Anna's grandpa would regale her and inspire her to stay focused and motivated. As the final exam dates drew closer, Anna's family created a conducive study environment for her, minimizing distractions and ensuring she had everything she needed to concentrate, with her family's love and support. Anna felt invincible; she was confident that she could achieve her dream of becoming a doctor. Anna knew that she was one step closer to making her dreams a reality. As the school days drew to a close, Anna couldn't help but feel a mix of emotions while her classmates were buzzing with excitement about the upcoming farewell ceremony. Anna's mind was preoccupied with the final exams and the medical entrance exam that was just around the corner.

Anna had always been a focused and driven student, and she knew that she had to stay concentrated if she wanted to achieve her dream of becoming a doctor. She had worked hard throughout the year, and she was determined to give it her all in the remaining exams.

As she walked through the school corridors, Anna couldn't help but feel a pang of sadness. She had spent so many years in schooling, and especially these 2 years of higher secondary, she had created so many wonderful memories with her friend, Sophia. They had shared laughter, tears, and countless moments of joy, and Anna knew that she would miss Sophia dearly once they parted ways.

Anna's classmates, on the other hand, seemed to be in a frenzy about the farewell ceremony. They were all chatting excitedly about what they would organize. Anna listened to their conversation with a mixture of detachment and curiosity. She was happy for them, but she couldn't help but feel like she was already moving on to the next chapter of her life.

As the days went by, Anna found herself feeling increasingly nostalgic. She knew that she would miss her school life dearly, but she was also excited about the future. She was eager to take the next step, to pursue her dreams, and to make a difference in the world. She knew that she was ready for whatever lay ahead.

With her final exams finally behind her, Anna felt a sense of relief wash over her. She had worked hard throughout the year, and she was confident that she had done her best. Now all she could do was wait for the exam results, which would determine her future. But Anna wasn't one to sit idle. She knew that the medical entrance exam was just around the corner, and she was determined to give it her all. She had always dreamed of becoming a doctor, and she was willing to put in the hard work necessary to achieve her goal.

As the holidays began, Anna took a decisive step towards realizing her dream of becoming a doctor. She joined a renowned academy that specialized in preparing students for medical entrance exams.

The academy was known for its rigorous training program. Which pushed students to their limits and beyond.

CHAPTER FIVE

THE CRACKS BEGIN

Anna was aware that the process would be challenging, but she was determined to give it her all. She bid farewell to her family and settled into the academy's hostel, ready to immerse herself in the intensive training to crack the medical entrance exam. The training was indeed grueling. Anna's days began at 3AM, with a quick marathon study session that lasted until 10PM. The academy's instructors were demanding, pushing the students to their limits.

To add to the challenge, the academy had a strict no-mobile-phone policy, and students were not allowed to communicate with their parents or friends until the exam date. Anna found this particularly tough, as she was used to being in constant touch with her family. But she knew that this was a necessary sacrifice if she wanted to achieve her goal. Despite the tough schedule and strict rules, Anna thrived in the academy's environment. She was surrounded by like-minded students who shared their passion for medicine, and the instructors were knowledgeable and supportive. Anna began to feel the effects of the intense training program; she was getting less sleep, and the constant pressure to perform was taking a toll on her mental health. But she refused to give up, drawing on her inner reserves of strength and determination to push through the tough times.

Anna's family, meanwhile, was anxiously waiting to hear from her. They had been instructed not to contact her until the exam date, but they couldn't help feeling a little worried about their daughter. They knew that Anna was strong and capable, but they also knew that the academy's program was notoriously tough.

As the exam date drew closer, Anna's family could only wait and pray that their daughter would emerge victorious; they knew that Anna had given it her all, and they were confident that she would make them proud.

As the days went by, Anna was deeply immersed in her studies at the academy, preparing for the medical entrance exam. She had been making good progress, and her instructors were confident that she would do well.

But then, one day, Anna received an unexpected instruction from the academy authorities. They told her that she needed to leave immediately to visit her grandfather, who was seriously ill. Anna was taken aback by the news, and her mind went blank. She had always been close to her grandfather, and the thought of losing him was unbearable. Anna's life came to a standstill as she struggled to process the news. She felt like she was in a daze, unable to think or react.

Anna finally mustered the courage to visit her grandfather. She was nervous and anxious, not knowing what to expect, when she arrived at her grandfather's bedside. She was shocked by his frail condition. He looked weak and tired, and Anna could see the pain in his eyes.

Anna was clueless about what to do or say. She felt like she was losing her grip on reality. She had always been a strong and determined person, but now she felt helpless and vulnerable. She sat beside her grandfather, holding his hand, and trying to process the emotions that were swirling inside her. As she looked at her grandfather, Anna felt a deep sense of sadness and loss. She knew that she might not have much time left with him, and the thought was almost too much to bear. She felt like her world was crumbling around her, and she didn't know how to pick up the pieces.

After visiting her grandfather, Anna's family tried to convince her to return to the academy to prepare for the exam, which was just round the corner, but Anna was resolute in her refusal; she couldn't bear the thought of leaving her grandfather's side, not even for a moment.

Her family tried to reason with her, explaining that she had worked so hard for this exam and that it was a crucial step towards realizing her dreams. But Anna was unmoved. Her grandfather's condition had shaken her to the core, and she couldn't think about anything else.

As the hours ticked by, Anna became increasingly withdrawn. She stopped thinking about the exam, her studies, and her future. All she could think about was her grandpa and how she could help him recover. She felt like she was in a state of denial, unable to accept the fact that her grandpa's condition was deteriorating. Anna's only thought was to be with her grandfather, to hold his hand, and to talk to him. She felt like she needed to be there for him, to support him, and to help him get better. The thought of losing him is unbearable, and she couldn't imagine a world without him. As the exam date drew closer. Anna's family grew increasingly worried. They knew how much this exam meant to Anna, and they didn't want her to throw away her chances. But Anna was adamant. She would go to the exam on the day of the exam, but she wouldn't leave her grandfather's side until then.

Anna's family eventually gave up trying to convince her, realizing that she needed to be with her grandfather during this difficult time. They stayed by her side, supporting her and her grandfather, and praying for a miracle.

Despite her prayers, her grandpa's health had continued to deteriorate, and it had become clear that his time was running out.

The day before her exam, Anna's worst fears were confirmed. Her grandfather passed away, surrounded by his loved ones. Anna was devastated, and she fainted from the shock and grief. Anna's heart was heavy with sorrow; she felt like a part of her had been torn away, and she couldn't imagine living without her grandfather.

She had missed her exam, but she didn't care on that day. She knew that her grandfather was gone and that nothing else mattered. The whole family was consumed by grief, and they came together to support each other through this difficult time. They attended the funeral, and Anna delivered a heartfelt eulogy, paying tribute to the man who had meant so much to her.

As they said their final goodbyes, Anna felt like she was losing a part of herself. She had never felt such a deep sense of loss and sadness before, and she didn't know how she would cope without her grandfather. But as she looked around at her family, she knew that she was not alone and that they would all get through this together.

The loss of her grandfather was Anna's second major heartbreak, coming after the death of her father. The pain and grief she felt were overwhelming, and she became mentally unstable, struggling to cope with the loss for two days. Anna was in a daze, unable to process her emotions or think clearly. She was consumed by grief, and her mind was a jumble of memories, regrets, and what-ifs.

But as the initial shock began to wear off, Anna's thoughts turned to the exam she had missed. She had worked so hard to prepare for it, and now it was gone, lost in the midst of her grief.

Anna felt a wave of sadness wash over her as she realized what she had missed. She had been so focused on her grandpa's illness and then his passing that she hadn't even thought about the exam. Now it was too late, and she couldn't help but wonder what could have been. As she sat in her room, surrounded by memories of her grandpa, Anna felt a deep sense of regret and loss. She had lost not only her grandfather but also her chance to take the exam. It was a double blow, and Anna didn't know how she would recover.

She had accidentally missed the exam to become a doctor, a dream she had held dear for so long. The realization hit her like a ton of bricks, and she became quiet, withdrawn, and lost.

For months, Anna cried, unable to accept the continuous heartbreaks she had suffered. She had lost her father, her grandpa, and now her chance to become a doctor. She felt like she was drowning in a sea of grief, and she didn't know how to keep her head above water.

Anna ignored everyone, including her mother, who tried to reach out to her. She felt empty, hollow, and lost, like a part of her had been ripped away. She stopped taking care of herself, starving and crying herself to sleep every night.

Her mother worried about Anna's well-being, tried to talk to her, to reach out to her, and bring her back from the brink. Anna's mother looked at her with tears in her eyes and said, "Anna, I know it's hard, but you have to move on. You can't let your dreams die with your grandfather.

He would want you to keep going, to chase your dreams, no matter what. You are strong, Anna, and you can get through this. I am here for you, and I will support you every step of the way.

Anna listened to her mother's words, feeling a glimmer of hope for the first time in months. With a heavy heart, she slowly began to try to move on, to find a new path, a new dream to chase. It wouldn't be easy, but with her mother's support, she knew she could face whatever came next.

On one random day, As Anna was in her house, still reeling from the loss of her grandpa, she heard a knock on the door. She got up to open it, and her face lit up with a weak smile as she saw Sophie standing in the doorway. Sophie hugged Anna tightly and said,. "I had no idea; I would have come earlier if I had known." Anna smiled weakly, feeling a sense of gratitude towards her friend.

"It's okay, Sophie; I know you would have come if you could."

"Anna, I have some news to share with you," Sophie said, her voice hesitant. "I've been accepted into a university abroad for my higher studies; I'll be leaving in a few days."

Anna's eyes widened in surprise; she was happy for Sophie. She smiled and hugged Sophie. This is an amazing opportunity for you.

You deserve it, As they hugged, Anna felt a sense of bittersweetness. She was happy for Sophie's success, but she knew that she would miss her friend terribly.

CHAPTER SIX

LIFE'S FIRST LESSONS

With a newfound determination, Anna and her mother decided to explore alternative options for her education. They discovered that Anna's grades and qualifications made her a strong candidate for admission to Engineering College. Anna's mother, seeing the spark of determination in her daughter's eyes, encouraged her to pursue this new path. Anna, though initially hesitant, eventually agreed to join the engineering college.

As the day of departure approached, Anna felt a mix of emotions; she was excited to start this new chapter of her life, but she was also sad to leave her home and her mother behind. She had thought of adjusting to hostel life as daunting. But Anna was determined to make the most of this opportunity; she packed her bags, said goodbye to her tearful mother, and set off for the Engineering College. As she settled into her new life in the hostel, Anna felt a sense of liberation and independence. She was ready to take on this new challenge and make a fresh start, but Anna was quite disturbed by this new environment.

The hostel room, though small and simple, felt like a new world to Anna; she was sharing the room with her three roommates, and all of them were friendly and welcoming. As they introduced themselves and started chatting, Anna felt a sense of belonging and camaraderie that she had been missing for a long time. As she lay in the bed that night, listening to the sounds of the hostel and the chatter of her new friends, Anna felt a sense of hope and renewal. She knew that this was just the beginning of a new journey, one that would be filled with its own set of challenges and opportunities, but for now, she was content to take things one step at a time and to see where this new path would lead her. As Anna settled into her new life in the hostel, she faced a mix of emotions. On. On one hand, she was excited to start the new chapter of her life and make new friends. On the other hand, she was struggling to cope with the loss of her grandpa and medical life and the stress of adjusting to a new environment. Anna felt overwhelmed by the sheer number of people and the constant din of chatter and laughter. She longed for the peace and quiet of her home, where she could retreat to her room and be alone with her thoughts.

Despite the challenges, Anna was determined to make the most of her time in the hostel. She started attending classes; she met new people, made friends, and slowly began to feel more at home.

However, there were still tough days. Days when the loneliness and grief felt like too much to bear. Days when Anna just wanted to curl up in her bed and cry. But she couldn't give in to those feelings. She had to keep moving forward, for her own sake and for the sake of her grandpa's memory.

But most of all, Anna missed the pampering; she missed the way her mother would fuss over her, making sure she was eating well, sleeping well, and studying hard; she even missed her sister Rachel. She often talks to her mom and sister via mobile. One day Anna's roommate, a girl named Alice, approached her as she was sitting in their room, staring blankly at her books. Alice asked Anna if she was okay, and Anna broke down in tears. Alice listened patiently as Anna poured out her heart, sharing her feelings of loss and loneliness. From that day on, Alice became Anna's support system. They would talk for hours, sharing hopes and dreams, their fears and insecurities.

Alice helped Anna to see that she wasn't alone, that everyone in the hostel was struggling with their own issues. Anna slowly began to heal. She started to enjoy her time. As Anna walked across the university campus, her feet carried her towards her classes, but her mind wandered to a different dream. She had always wanted to be a doctor, to help people, to make a difference in their lives. But life had taken a different turn, and she found herself studying engineering instead.

As she sat in her lectures, Anna's eyes would glaze over, and she would imagine herself in a white coat, stethoscope around her neck, diagnosing patients and prescribing treatments. She would think about the thrill of saving lives, of being a part of something bigger than herself.

But the sound of the professor's voice would snap her back to reality, and Anna would feel a pang of disappointment and frustration. Why couldn't she pursue her true passion? Why did she have to settle for something else?

As she walked out of the classroom, Anna would feel a sense of disconnect, like she was living someone else's dream. She would wonder what her life would be like if she had taken a different path, if she had followed her heart instead of her head.

Despite her doubts, Anna knew she couldn't give up; she had to make the most of the opportunities she had and find ways to connect her passion. Anna was determined to find a way to make her dreams a reality. But as the days went by, Anna felt lonely, but at least she had one friend in this sea of unfamiliar faces. She and Alice would talk and hang out, but Anna longed for more. She wanted to be a part of a group, to feel like she belonged. But every time she tried to join a conversation or participate in a class discussion, she would freeze up and feel like an outsider.

One day, as they both were sitting in the hostel corridor, they noticed a group of students laughing and chatting together. They seemed to be having so much fun, and Anna and Alice felt a pang of envy; why couldn't they be part of a group like that?

They both started thinking of joining in that squad of friends.

As they started talking with them, Anna realized they were the friends she longed for. Anna became more friendly with those people, feeling like she had finally found her place.

Anna felt a sense of excitement and belonging; Anna and Alice's friendship was a beautiful one. But as time went on, things started to change. Anna began to drift away from Alice and spent more and more time with a new group of friends. She felt Alice alone; days went by, each with the other handing the time of her life with her new gang of friends. It was as if they had both decided to mind their own business and focus on their friendship. As time went on, the unspoken tension between them began to simmer just as the clashes started. As the clashes escalated, it became clear that the feud between Alice and Anna was far from over. Anna's new friends were a big part of her healing process. They were supporting understanding. She was finally starting to move on from the loss of her grandpa and the disappointment of not being able to pursue her medical dreams. Anna was thrilled to have found her tribe, and she felt like she was finally starting to settle into college life. However, as the weeks went by, Anna started to feel a nagging sense of guilt. She had come to college with a clear goal in mind: to study hard, get good grades, and secure a bright future for herself. Anna realized that she had lost sight of her original goal. She was wasting her time by procrastinating, putting off assignments until the last minute, and spending too much time socializing. Anna felt like she was stuck in a rut, and she didn't know how to get out of it. One day, as she was sitting in her room, staring blankly at her family photo, Anna had an epiphany; she realized that she had been so focused on having fun and making friends that she had forgotten why she came to college. Anna felt a surge of determination and motivation. she knows that she needed to get her priorities straight and start focusing on her studies again. She made a promise to herself to buckle down, stay organized, and make the most of her time in college with a new sense of purpose. Anna dove back into her studies, determined to make the most of her college experience. She was ready to work hard, stay focused, and achieve her goals.

Anna found herself struggling to keep up with her engineering coursework. Despite attending her classes. She would sit in class, feeling like her brain was turning to mush.

Anna's academic performance began to suffer. Her grades began to slip, and she found herself feeling anxious and stressed about her academic performance. Anna took a deep breath and let the thought sink in, "Engineering is not my cup of tea, but I have to make it."

Anna and her friends were all concerned about their studies and spending more and more time on their own, trying to keep up with their coursework. As a result, the time they spent together as a group began to dwindle. At first, it was just a matter of everyone being busy and not having as much time to hang out. Anna started to notice that her friends were forming new connections, and Anna was being left behind. As the gang slowly disbanded, Anna found Alice; she had abandoned Alice, ignored her, and left her feeling hurt, experiencing the same pain and rejection that she had inflicted on Alice. Anna's eyes widened as she realized that karma was indeed a boomerang. What she had done to Alice had come back to her in return. Anna felt a wave of regret wash over her.

Anna realized that she had deserved to be left behind by her friends. She thought about the time she ignored Alice and made her feel like she wasn't important. As Anna reflected on her past behavior, she felt a deep sense of remorse. She knew that she had hurt someone she cared about and that she had damaged a beautiful friendship. She wished she could go back and do things differently, but she knew that was impossible. All Anna could do now was learn from her mistakes and try to become a better person. She vowed to be more empathetic, more compassionate, and more loyal to her friends.

She knew that it couldn't be easy to repair the damage she had done, but she was willing to try; despite her trying, the pain and heartache she had endured had taken a toll on her mental health, leaving her shattered and broken. The loneliness had created a perfect storm of emotional turmoil.

Anna navigated the challenges of adulting; she found herself becoming increasingly weird, arrogant, and sensitive. She had always been a happy and carefree kid, but the hardship she had faced had changed her.

Anna felt like she was drowning in a sea of despair, with no lifeline in sight. She cried herself to sleep at night, her tears falling silently onto her pillow as she mourned the loss of her innocence and her happiness. She felt unloved and unwanted, like she was a burden to those who were around her.

Anna felt like she was losing herself, like she was disappearing into darkness. She didn't know how to find her way back to the happy, carefree kid she used to be once.

And so, Anna's journey continued, a journey of healing.

CHAPTER SEVEN

BREAKING FREE!!

The sweet and loving Anna, who had once been a beacon of warmth and kindness, had begun to wither away. The pain and heartache she had endured had slowly turned her into a shadow of her former self. She had started to hate everyone, and the world seemed like a cold and unforgiving place. It was a stark contrast to the Anna of old, who had been raised with love and affection.

She had always been a lovable and pampered kid, surrounded by people who adored her. As a result, Anna had grown up with a heart full of love and trust. She had always seen the best in people and had easily formed close bonds with those around her.

But now, the wounds of her current phase had left her feeling faded and cylindrical.

Anna had begun to question everyone's motives, and she felt like she was walking on eggshells, never knowing when someone would hurt her again. As she navigated the world with her newfound hatred and mistrust, Anna couldn't help but feel a pang of sadness; she missed the carefree and loving person she used to be. She missed the way she used to see the world, full of hope and possibility. But most of all, Anna missed the connections she used to have with others.

She missed the laughter, the sense of belonging that came with having close friends. Now, she felt like she was alone in a crowded room, surrounded by people who seemed to be moving further and further away from her.

Anna's heart ached as she realized that she had lost herself in the process of trying to protect herself from getting hurt again. She had built walls around herself. Walls that were meant to keep people out, but that also kept her from experiencing the beauty of human connection.

The weight of self-doubt had begun to bear down on Anna, suffocating her with its crushing grip. She had started to question her own worth, wondering if she was even deserving of love and affection. The negative self-talk had become a constant companion, whispering cruel lies into her ear. "You're not good enough," it would say, "You're not lovable."

"You're not worthy of happiness."

Anna would try to shake off these thoughts, but they seemed to be wiser, poisoning her mind and heart. She began to feel like she was walking through a dense fog, unable to see her own value or worth.

As she looked in the mirror, Anna saw a stranger staring back at her. She didn't recognize the person she had become, a person who was consumed by self-doubt and negativity. The pain led Anna to believe that she was unlovable, that she didn't deserve to be happy. She felt like she was broken, like she was beyond repair.

As the days went by, Anna's self-doubt only grew stronger. She had begun to withdraw from the world, afraid of being hurt again. She felt like she was living in a prison of her own making, with no escape in sight.

The once-confident and carefree Anna was now a shadow of her former self. She was lost and alone, struggling to find her way back to the light.

Anna's inferiority complex had grown exponentially, casting a dark shadow over her entire being. She felt like she was worthless, like she was fit for nothing; every day she woke up with a sense of dread, feeling like she was a burden to those around her. Anna had always been clingy and expected them to reciprocate the love and attention she showered upon her friends.

Despite being a stubborn and overindulged kid, Anna had never intentionally hurt anyone. She had always come from a place of love, just a friendly, fiercely in return. But now she felt like she was paying the price of her own naivety. Anna's habit of expecting reciprocation had ultimately led to her downfall. She had given her heart and soul to her friends, expecting them to do the same in return.

But when they didn't, Anna felt like she was left with nothing. As she wandered through her empty days, Anna couldn't help but wonder if she was worthy of love at all; she felt like she was a constant disappointment to those around her, like she was a failure in every sense of the word. The pain of her rejection had cut deep, leaving Anna feeling like she was bleeding from the inside out.

She didn't know how to heal the wounds that had been inflicted upon her. All Anna knew was that she was hurting and that she didn't know how to stop the pain. She felt like she was drowning in a sea of despair, with no lifeline in sight.

The dam had finally burst, and Anna's emotions came flooding out. She had been holding it all in for so long, trying to keep up a brave face, but the pain and sadness had become too much to bear. She burst out crying great sobs racking her body as she released all the pent-up emotions.

Her friends, who had been keeping their distance, were shocked and concerned when they heard about Anna's breakdown. They immediately dropped everything and rushed to her side, surrounding her with love and support.

As they hugged her and stroked her hair, Anna felt a wave of relief wash over her.

She had been so alone for so long, and it felt amazing to have her friends back by her side. They listened to her as she poured out her heart, telling them about all the pain and sadness she had been feeling as they consoled her. Anna's friends realized that they had taken her for granted.

They had assumed that she would always be there for them, but they had neglected to be there for her when she needed them most. The friendship was reunited, but it was different now. The dynamics had shifted, and they all knew that things couldn't go back to the way they were before they had grown and learned from their experiences, and their friendship had been tempered by the fires of adversity.

Anna's friends made a conscious effort to be more supportive and understanding, to be there for her in ways they hadn't been before.

And Anna, for her part, learned to communicate her needs and feelings more effectively, to not assume that her friends would automatically know what she was going through.

The reunion was a new beginning, a chance for them to rebuild their friendship on a stronger, more empathetic foundation. It wasn't the same as it had been before, but it was better, deeper, and more meaningful.

As Anna reflected on her experiences, she realized that the past year of hostel life had been a transformative journey for her. At just 17 years old, she had faced challenges and hardships that had forced her to grow up and learn valuable lessons about life. Anna's eyes sparkled with a newfound wisdom as she declared, "Hostel life has taught me more in one year than my 16 years of pampered life ever could."

She had discovered that the world was not always a comfortable and predictable place and that sometimes, you had to face difficulties head-on in order to grow.

The pampered life she had led before had shielded her from many of the harsh realities of the world. But hostel life had thrown her into a melting pot of different personalities, experiences, and challenges, forcing her to adapt and learn.

Anna realized that she had been naïve and sheltered before, but that hostel life had opened her eyes to the complexities and nuances of human relationships. She had learned to navigate conflicts, to empathize with others, and to find her own voice in a crowded and often chaotic world. As she looked back on her journey.

Anna felt a sense of pride and accomplishment; she had forced her fears. Overcome obstacles and emerged stronger and wiser as a result. The lessons she had learned in hostel life would stay with her forever, shaping her into a resilient, compassionate, and confident individual.

Anna's journey had finally led her to a profound realization. She had come to understand that she couldn't expect love to be reciprocated in the same way that she gave it. This epiphany had been a long time coming, but it was a crucial step in her growth from a pampered kid to a mature adult.

As she reflected on her relationships, Anna realized that her mom was the one person who had always reciprocated her love unconditionally. Her mom's unwavering support and affection had been a constant source of comfort and strength for Anna.

With this newfound understanding, Anna began to shift her focus away from seeking validation from others and towards her own goals and aspirations. She had always been driven to succeed, but now she had a renewed sense of purpose and motivation.

Anna's desire to make her mom proud became a powerful driving force in her life. She threw herself into her studies and was determined to achieve her goals and make a name for herself.

As she worked towards her objectives, Anna found that she was slowly healing from the wounds of her past.

The pain of her friendship breakup was still there, but it was no longer debilitating. She had learned to channel her emotions into positive action, and she was emerging stronger and more resilient as a result. Anna's transformation was nothing short of remarkable. She had faced her fears, overcome her insecurities, and discovered a newfound sense of purpose and direction.

As she looked to the future, Anna knew that she was ready for whatever challenges lay ahead. She was a young woman on a mission, driven by a fierce determination to succeed and make her mom proud. For Anna, friendship had become a mere formality.

The pain and heartache she had experienced in her past relationships had left her wary of getting too close to others. She had built walls around herself, walls that were meant to protect her from getting hurt again. As a result, Anna's friendships had become superficial and transactional.

She would go through the motions of being a good friend, attending social events and participating in group conversations, but she wouldn't truly invest her emotions or vulnerability in the relationships. Anna's friends, in turn, had begun to sense her emotional unavailability. They would try to get closer to her, to break down the walls she had built, but Anna would push them away. She was afraid of getting hurt again, afraid of being vulnerable and open with others.

In the end, Anna's friendships had become a mere formality, a social nicety that she maintained out of obligation rather than genuine affection. She was lonely and disconnected, stuck in a cycle of superficial relationships that brought her no joy or fulfillment. The irony of it all. When Anna finally let go of her expectation, she found happiness with her friends. She realized that she didn't need them to reciprocate her feelings in the same way or to meet her every emotional need. Simply being with them, communicating with them, and sharing experiences together was enough. The friendship breakup had been a painful but valuable lesson for Anna. She had learned that she didn't have to take everything personally, that not everyone would like her or appreciate her in the same way, and that was okay with her newfound understanding. Anna approached her friendships with a sense of freedom and lightness. She no longer felt the need to constantly seek validation or affirmation from her friends. She was happy to simply be with them, to enjoy their company, and to share in their joys and sorrows. Communication became the key to her relationships; Anna learned to express herself cleanly and honestly without expectations or attachment. She listened to her friends without judgment, and she offered support and encouragement when they needed it. In the end, Anna's friendships became more authentic and meaningful. She had learned to appreciate the beauty of imperfection and to accept that relationships are complex and multifaceted. And she had discovered that true happiness comes from within, from a place of self-acceptance and self-love. As the days turned into weeks, Anna's life continued to unfold in new and exciting ways at the end of her college life.

A NEW PATH UNFOLDS

Anna started to work hard, her hard work paid off, and she graduated. The job offers started pouring in, and Anna was thrilled to accept a position at one of the best companies in the industry. Anna stepped out of the hostel gates feeling a mix of emotions: excitement for the new chapter ahead, sadness for leaving behind her friends and the memories they shared, and a hint of nervousness about the unknown. As she looked back at the hostel building, she remembered the moments her friends had offered her. As they said their final goodbyes, Anna felt a sense of determination wash over her. She was ready to start the new chapter, armed with the lessons. She learned with a deep breath; Anna turned and walked away from the hostel, towards the bright future waiting for her. She was excited for her new job. Finally she was living her dream, and she felt an overwhelming sense of pride and accomplishment. As Anna settled into her new career, she began to drift apart from her college friends. They had all gone their separate ways, chasing their own dreams and aspirations. Anna would occasionally meet up with them for reunions or social events, but the connection was no longer the same.

Anna had grown older, and her priorities had shifted. She was now focused on building a successful career, and she didn't have the same amount of time or energy to devote to her social life. She had become more introspective, more focused on her own goals and aspirations. Despite the distance that had grown between her and her college friends, Anna was grateful for the experiences they had shared. She knew that those friendships had played a significant role in shaping her into the person she was today. And even though they were no longer a part of her daily life, Anna knew that she would always treasure the memories they had made together. Anna's excitement for the new chapter ahead, sadness for leaving behind her friends and the memories they shared, and a hint of nervousness about the unknown. Her friends, Rachel, stood beside her, beaming with pride and a tinge of sadness. They had been inseparable since their first year in college, and now they were about to embark on separate journeys. Anna's career was flourishing, and she was loving every minute of it. She had landed a job at a prestigious company, and her hard work and dedication had earned her a reputation as a rising star in her field.

Meanwhile, Rachel was also doing exceptionally well in her own career. She had started her own business, and it was taking off in a big way. She was working tirelessly to build her brand and expand her customer base. Their mother, Jane, couldn't be prouder of her two daughters. She had always known that they were capable of great things, and now she was getting to see them thrive in their respective careers. As a result of their success, Jane was enjoying a happy and comfortable lifestyle. She no longer had to worry about making ends meet, and she was able to indulge in her hobbies and interests without financial stress. Anna and Rachel made sure to spoil their mother rotten, taking her on vacations, buying her gifts, and spending quality time with her.

They knew that she had sacrificed a lot for them when they were growing up, and they wanted to show their appreciation for everything she had done for them. One day, Anna and Rachel decided to give their mother a luxury life. So, they pooled their resources and bought her a beautiful new home, complete with all the amenities she could ever want. Mrs. Jane was overwhelmed with emotion when she had never imagined that her daughter would be able to provide for her in such a way. "I'm so proud of you both," she said, tears streaming down her face. Anna and Rachel hugged their mother tightly, feeling happy and fulfilled knowing that they were able to make her life better. As the years passed, Anna and Rachel continued to work hard and build successful careers.

Rachel eventually met a kind and gentle man named Peter after certain months of being best friends. They got married in a beautiful ceremony, surrounded by friends and family. Peter was a wonderful son-in-law, treating Mrs. Jane with the same love and respect as his own mother. The family was overjoyed to have him as a part of their lives.

Anna, on the other hand, had become increasingly dependent on her mother. She had given up on the idea of getting married, feeling that she didn't need anyone else to complete her life. Her mother was her rock, and she was content with just having her by her side. However, fate had other plans. One day, while attending a family gathering, Anna met a kind and gentle man named Jaden.

He was warm, caring, and had a heart of gold. As they talked, Anna felt a deep connection to him, sensing that he was someone special. Over the next few years, Anna and Jaden spent more time together, and he found himself falling deeply in love with her. He was everything she had been missing in her life—a father figure, a partner, and a best friend. Jaden proposed to Anna a few days later, and she said yes without hesitation. They got married in a beautiful, intimate ceremony, surrounded by their close friends and family. As they exchanged their vows, Anna felt a sense of completeness she had never felt before. She knew that she had found her soulmate in Jaden and that he would love and cherish her for the rest of her life. The family was overjoyed to welcome Jaden into their lives, and Mrs. Jane was thrilled to see her daughters happy and in love. As they all hugged and celebrated, Anna knew that she had finally found her happily ever after. Anna had been living a comfortable and happy life with her loving husband. Jaden, she had a successful career, a beautiful home, and a loving family.

However, one day, as she was going about her daily routine, she suddenly felt an intense longing for something she had left behind. As she had always dreamed of becoming a doctor, but life had taken her on a different path. Anna couldn't shake off the feeling of nostalgia and longing that had washed over her. She felt a sudden urge to wear that doctor's coat again, to feel the sense of purpose and fulfillment that came with being a doctor. She tried to brush off the feeling, telling herself that she had made the right choices in life. But the longing persisted, and Anna couldn't help but wonder what her life would have been like if she had pursued her dream of becoming a doctor. As the days went by, Anna found herself spending more and more time thinking about her abandoned medical career. She began to question whether she had made a mistake by giving up on her dreams.

Jaden noticed the change in Anna's behavior and approached her one evening, "Hey, what's been on your mind lately?" he asked, concern etched on his face. Annan hesitated, unsure of how to express her feelings. "I don't know, Jaden." I just feel like something is missing. I keep thinking about my medical career and wondering what could have been. Jaden listened attentively, his eyes filled with understanding. "Maybe it's not too late to explore that passion again," he suggested gently. Anna's eyes widened as she considered the possibility. Anna's decision to pursue a medical career was met with unwavering support from Jaden. He encouraged her to take the leap, reminding her of dreams with renewed determination. Anna enrolled in medical college, eager to start her journey. The next few years were a whirlwind of intense studying, long hours, and clinical rotations.

Despite the challenges, Anna persevered, driven by her passion for medicine and her desire to make a difference in people's lives. Jaden was her support system, providing emotional support and helping her balance the demands of medical college. Finally, after half a decade of hard work, Anna graduated with her medical degree. The sense of pride and accomplishment she felt was overwhelming as she walked across the stage with her graduation certificate in hand.

As she looked out at the sea of faces, Anna's eyes met Jaden's, and she smiled, knowing that she couldn't have done it without him. Her husband beamed with pride, tears of joy welling up in his eyes. Anna embarked on her residency, eager to put her knowledge and skills into practice and impact her patients lives, and she knew that she had the support of her loved ones every step of the way. Years later, Anna had established herself as a respected and compassionate doctor, known for her exceptional manner and her dedication to her patients. She looked back on her journey, grateful for the twists and turns that had led her to where she was meant to be. As Anna spoke, her voice trembled with emotion, and tears of joy streamed down her face.

Jaden's eyes welled up with tears as well, and he took Anna's hands in his, holding them tightly. "My love, you deserve all the love in the world," Jaden said, his voice choked with emotion, "I'm just grateful to be the one to give it to you.

You're an amazing woman, Anna, and I'm so proud of everything you've accomplished." Anna smiled through her tears, feeling a deep sense of gratitude and love for her husband. She knew that she had found her soulmate in Jaden and that he would always be there to support and love her.

"You're the best, Jaden," Anna said, her voice barely above a whisper. "You too, Anna." Jaden replied, and with Jaden by her side, Anna finally experienced the paternal love she had missed out on. Jaden's love and acceptance helped Anna heal from the wounds of her past, and she began to see herself in a new light. Jane's presence in her life had brought her a sense of joy, peace, and belonging that she had never thought possible. At last, Anna closed her eyes, took a deep breath, and thanked God for this beautiful life. She knew that she had been blessed with so much, and she was grateful for every moment. Every laugh and every tear," and she was excited to see what the future held.

"THE END"

MOLLYCODDLE

--- *CATHERINE NITHISHA*